A short collection of poems where

THE GLASS IS HALF EMPTY

A short collection of poems where

THE GLASS IS HALF EMPTY

Madhuri Suma

Bigfoot Publications
Because, there's a writer in everyone.

A short collection of poems where
THE GLASS IS HALF EMPTY
Author : Madhuri Suma

First Published by
Bigfoot06 Publications (OPC) Pvt. Ltd.
1st floor, BSR Building near Vishal Mega Mart,
Daultabad Flyover, Laxman Vihar Phase 3,
Gurugram, Haryana (122001)
Website: www.bigfootpublications.in
Email: info@bigfootpublications.in

First Edition : December, 2023

ISBN Print Book -978-81-19512-94-2

Typeset in Garamond 12pt
by Yachika Prajapati For Bigfoot06 Publications

Printed in India

Dedicated to all the untainted hearts

Table of Contents

Social Chaos

Infinity

Introduction

The world can be a strikingly beautiful place. But beauty often coexists with its opposite, the ugliness, for the two to hold meaning in our lives. Each time I pointed out the things that probably weren't very "positive" with my art or my writing, I was always met with "you're too negative" or "Damn! You're such a pessimist". However, it's essential to recognize that pessimism is a philosophy—I, on the other hand, don't align myself with such a label. (If you want to delve into true pessimism, explore "The Conspiracy against Human Race" by Thomas Ligotti.)

I do however believe that I possess an ability to notice the world's murky facets that often go unnoticed by the 'optimists' around me. I believe the cause lies in my anxiety, although now cured, left traces and keeps me running with all the possible scenarios and observations.

"The Glass Is Half Empty" is not an exploration of pessimism; rather, it reflects my amateurish attempt to navigate my mind and share it with you. As someone naturally drawn to the not-so-happy aspects of life, this title serves as a mirror to my tendency to see challenges in order to appreciate beauty. Join me on this introspective journey where each verse becomes a canvas for embracing both shadows and light, revealing delight that emerges from the depths of my musings.

Acknowledgement

Thanks to everyone I have met and encountered in my life. Every brief encounter has been my source of inspiration and my creative stimulation.

Shadow Dance

For those acquainted with Carl Jung's work, the term "Shadow" holds a significant meaning. In the realm of Jungian psychology, the Shadow encompasses the aspects of our psyche, both positive and negative, that we repress. It harbours its own concealed personality within the depths of our consciousness, restrained from expression, yet capable of emerging like a formidable force.

This segment of the book delves into the realm of my shadow self. Some pieces are a result of free association, flowing directly from the depths of my subconscious. Others, though edited, emerged mysteriously, their origins and meanings unknown. This collection is a play with shadows, a manifestation of hidden layers, perhaps veiled miseries buried deep within me. As you explore these verses, you're invited to unravel the mysteries and confront the shadows that linger in the recesses of my mind

Demons

Welcome, Dear Incubus,

possessing every form of my love,

what do you wish to whore

with a shadow of your touch?

Feared the nights in your presence,

and the daylight as your lunch;

I swallow your supremacy,

as you can no longer hurt me,

what can you take from the one,

who has exhausted themselves and has none?

Balance

Watch me liquify in the heat

radiated by your broken soul,

Everything you touch, melts losing its form

and its originality without a figure;

Watch my remains,

the fundamentals of my being

push me towards an existential crisis,

as you blow away my ashes;

Watch my purity evaporate

into the void replicating your heart,

the innocence and my identity turning grim,

concluding me with nothing

Evil

You pour out of my shower, hit and miss my face,

Dancing on my tongue, when I bow down and pray,

The afforestation around me that you've planted;

Limiting my passage to love and life altogether,

The woodpecker in my chest that you pet,

Pricking my insides in shame;

And I dissolve like a pill in coffee with a residue of none,

And you trip in fear and satisfaction snorting my agony cocaine

Flickering light

The lack of colour around me,
perplexed, to know if I'm awake or asleep,
my body shuts down, have I always been a human?
failed attempt to move, have I forgotten
how to breathe, hear and speak?
Perhaps, I'm a rock beneath the sea
submerged and suffocated all along,
I must have dreamt of a life of motion,
a reality that has long gone;

My mobile vision finally captures a colour
of a seaweed taking a form, three eyes, and a head
its ugly body lying on top of my chest
handcuffs while I struggle to move
Whispers, "B*****! I'm going to consume you"
it smirks, flickering like a candle fire
I surrender in delight, but I finally open my eyes

Beach

My last night at the beach, the wind unusually loud,

The water rose higher than you and me,

Gulping down the peace it promised to bring;

I glance into the silver abyss,

While I birthed my nihilistic heart,

A realization that I will never be the same,

struck me when I looked at you all sane;

As the water sucked my soul through my feet,

You engulfed the remaining with a forced kiss;

The clouds now conceal the shame

of the sphere for revelations made too late;

I bodied with no attempt to struggle

as you and the ocean consumed my fate.

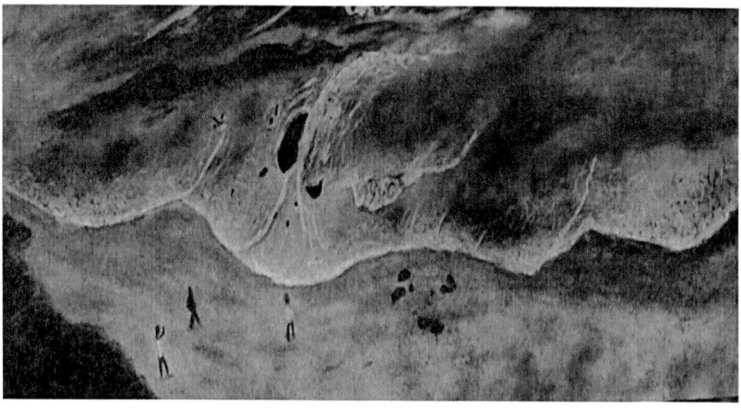

Shallow

I can't remember the scar on your face,

or your arm? It never mattered

I don't recollect what you look like,

until I Stumble upon your pictures,

Your voice a faint memory,

The same auditory

Wave in a crowded space;

Sorry, I don't remember your scent,

Or the warmth in your hug,

I'm shallow,

Only evidence of your existence clinging onto me

Is your broken soul,

Your destructive lies, that still lingers,

The unfortunate events in your presence,

And how I lost all I had, my faith, respect, and innocence.

Slut

Who am I?

The numbers, 34’ 28’, 38’

A length 5’8”

A figure Cornet A sl**

Prologue

My cornet figure sheds a layer

And detaches its legs

“Denude my soul”, the vulva begs;

But the lips are glutted,

Stripping dreams,

Disrobing reality;

As the soul excludes my body

The filth penetrates hastily,

His pride abandons my abyss

and my filthy lips plead

“DIE, you Sl**”

Prophecy

There's a loneliness within me,

an aching void that can't be filled.

I can't trace its source, so I name it:

heartbreak, hatred, anxious, lost?

But even when I try to surrender

or give it a name to hold,

the feeling lingers on, relentless,

a weight that can't be consoled.

Way Out

Change to blend with the surrounding,
Solid to liquid, liquid to solid
disoriented and fatigued,
I look outside the grey world
Oblivious to other's insights;
unable to accelerate, despite
the repairs I've made
maybe one day, I will see some colour
or maybe my vision will adapt to the gray
but I'll continue my attempts, oh misery,
even if you devour me as your prey

Wearying Anxiety

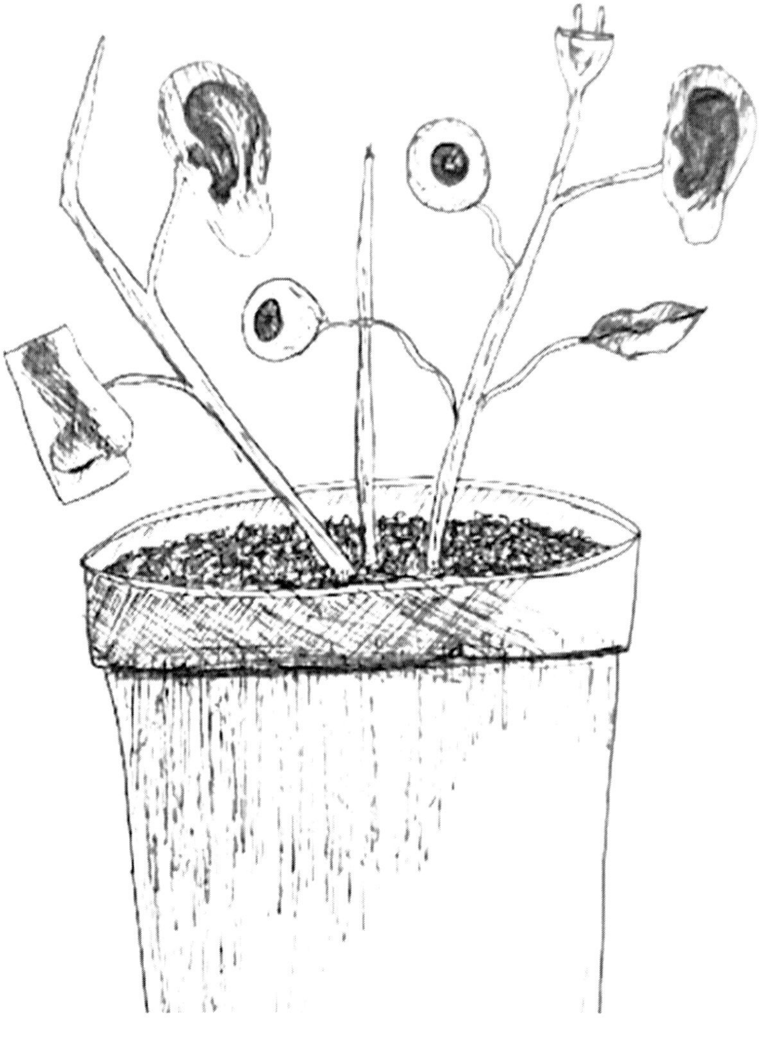

If there's one prominent quality of anxiety it is the ability to overthink and over analyse things. Although it might seem like something everyone does or a part of creative ability, this habit of over-analysis didn't seem to fade even when not followed by a racing heartbeat and a sick feeling in the stomach.

In this section, I delve into the intricacies of my thoughts that anxiety orchestrates. A symphony of random musings, some grounded in reality, while others are diversions of my own creation. Perhaps, at times, I've found solace in romanticising the melancholic, or maybe I'm merely captivated by the unnecessary amusement my mind formulates.

As you navigate through these writings, bear in mind that this is a freestyle association—an unfiltered exploration of my thoughts. The tangled threads you encounter here mirror the intricacies of an anxious mind, weaving a narrative that is as unpredictable as the currents of the restless sea.

Coffee

My eyes heavy and withdrawn,
soreness marks my body from working before dawn
Strain my legs with every move;
Despite the mail that reads "We care for you,"
hypnotized by the screens that demand,
more time than you can withstand;
Gently losing the accurate implication of job,
Forced obligations to stay with the mob;
Most of us can't discharge if tried,
because if you're employed, it's a fortunate life;
Call to mind, the last satisfying slumber,
the only remaining definition of pleasure

Some caffeine to silence my mental disputes,
acknowledging that I'm paid some residue,
which I use to fake a living
and to mask my dissatisfied "well-being"

Derealization

A faint heartbeat slowly fades,

as your vision splits to two,

See the whirl from the extreme of your eyes,

in this hideous act,

you watch yourself fight;

Master of the worlds you see,

Are you the animation or the audience perceiving?

Surrender

The monotonous air inhaled,

A rhythmic heartbeat on a minor scale,

The odour of familiarity combined,

Destroy the clocks and there's no time

Are we stagnant? Or in a loop?

Caressed by our unresolved disputes

Serenity devoured by silence,

Make a sound, at the least whisper,

to establish our presence.

Placebo

Distressed by change, and unidentified update,

why would you choose to stay

in your familiar comforting ache?

As my trembling foot raises to forward,

your fretfulness freezes it midair,

multiplying the terror of unacquainted,

carting any developed way

Your immobility in this rain,

Fractures my legs and arms,

demanding one ask,

"Tell me mind, do you wish to change?"

Traffic

The RBG in a teasing chase,

A river of white cars in a rapid race

Red fireflies at each car's tail

Adding colour to a world gone pale

Our Species morph into machines

Robots, unlike the movie screens

Wheels, now an extension of our feet,

Earphones, the sole street antenna we need.

In the city's lack of glow,

We blend with the city's doubtful traffic flow.

Taxi Ride

A mundane day on repeat,

The traffic lights playing tag

I look outside my taxi window

At a world morbid and black.

Each mind generates its own universe

While the bodies function on autopilot

Not a single one is in the moment

Fading awareness causes no torment.

Lethargic smoke forms the vehicles,

Collides with the pungent odour of distress

The streets are filled crowds and automobiles

Yet loneliness resides in most places

Perhaps, it's my dirty glasses that I see no colour,

Or I've looked through the collective confusion,

over the price we pay to justify our delusions.

Cleansing

Fire disguised as water,

Slipping by my skin,

like a satin bedsheet;

This neutral colour, paints crimson over my caramel brown,

The heat sank into my body, causing a mild ache,

"I must be a masochist to find pleasure this way;

"Dig deeper, love, and melt my unusual self"

I encounter my form disappear into the smoke,

Like in a cheap bar,

Paralyzed by the heat,

as I wait for the toxins to release;

Smirk at my own innocence,

"If only bathing washed away my reminiscence"

Distant

The clouds are a shade greyer than usual,

casting a mellow shadow on your resting body,

unable to detect your liquid life;

a numbness that separates me from all around,

Am I inhumane to not cry?

over the nothingness you want to convey?

The existence and morals that I request,

a result of losing love and feeling no emotion,

Perhaps there's no good, evil, right, and wrong,

Or maybe, I'm not capable of love and hate

Perhaps, there's no truth and no lie

And there's no winner and loser,

when the death comes by

Pattern

There's a silence between the noise

A haunting wave that dominates

hiding its whispers

Sneaking up on me

It paints my mind black

Why am I not used to its familiarity?

An inconvenient smirk,

Shooting my way,

here and there, and everywhere

trapped in a loop of confusion

Where is the escape or a change in the pattern?

The golden ratio of mishaps,

A bigger picture I fail to grasp,

Forcing yet another attempt,

to overlook reality and its contempt

Colour Wheel

I've looked in places of worship,

I've skimmed through multiple books,

I've played a thousand videos,

And some conversations on loop.

I've sought solace in a lover's embrace,

Intimacy from ancestry,

Witnessed friends oscillate,

Gulped coffees with acquaintances and colleagues.

I've tried a chemical to induce hallucinations,

And a pill to alleviate anxiety,

Also, some exercise to release happiness,

But where's the promised colour wheel?

I've changed the colour of my lens,

Yet the smudge I still see,

Everything's still so blurred and foggy,

Where's the promised colour wheel?

Cigarette

As you breathe the smoke out on my face,

Unaware of my existence,

Until I passive it,

Dreadfulness burns my passage on the way in;

How did it come to this?

I look at you and can't think of a reason to be friends,

We latch on to each other's shadows.

to feel less surreal among the other pets

of fate; complimenting each other's deepened senses,

Limping as our trust for the other bleeds,

I realize how puny I am when I see

you exhaust and toss away.

the cigarette, you would prefer over me any day.

Social Chaos

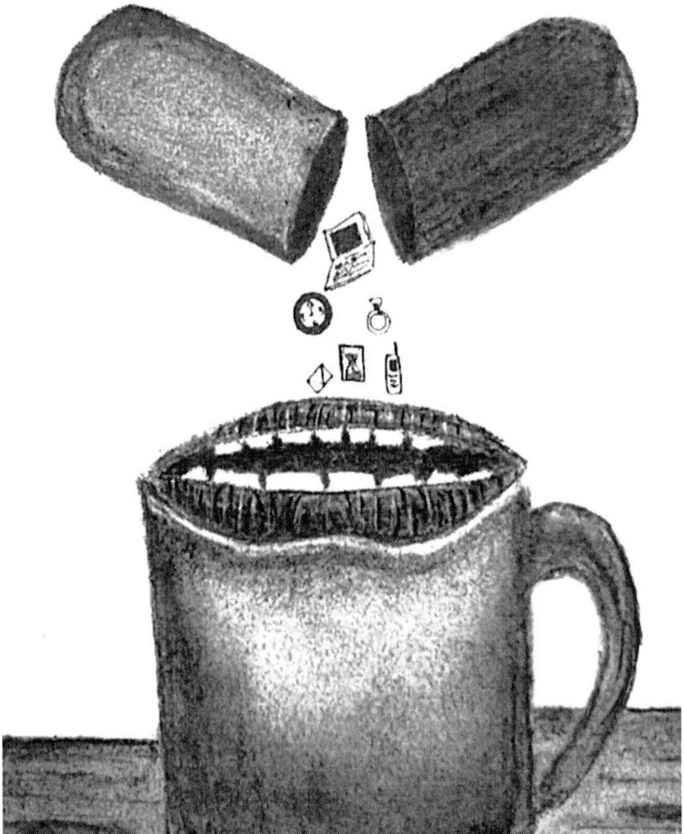

As introverts, we often find solace in observing the nuances of social dynamics, sometimes humorously critiquing, or exposing the underlying flaws. In the face of our perceived social shortcomings, our creative minds often fixate on the negative aspects of people and society, questioning the inherent selfishness that can permeate our interactions.

This collection of poems reflects those moments when social discomfort fuelled the creative process, giving rise to verses that unravel the complexities, absurdities, and sometimes, the beauty found in the chaos of social existence. So, brace yourself for an exploration of the social realm, as seen through the lens of an introverted observer.

The Crowd

Colourful shades submerge my foresight,
Distorting keen senses in a hurried pace.
The collective noise screams confusion,
as my Heartbeat leaks its distaste.

Deep within, my essence trembles,
Unable to flee or fight the unseen.
Prudence divorces fear,
Yet it lingers, unwavering, within me.

Murmurs of the crowd unite,
Evolving into a monster's growl.
Each breath I take cries,
Over the hypersensitivity's scowl.

Submit to the disquieting shadow,
For it's a demon deep and hollow.

Dear Humblebragger

Your eyes gleam with pride,
A smug grin upon your face
I roll my mind's eyes,
and conceal the distaste.

You boast of sorrows and hurdles,
The greatness of your will
Standing tall as if better than the rest
Looking down at our realistic distress.
Each word marinated in pride
Escapes with your egoistic smile
Crossing the line from confidence to humblebrag
All set to compete in the next lap.

Moving forward with your new flex,
From humblebrag to brag to a superiority complex.

No one is ahead of anyone in the race
Yet you yearn to win,
It has no end, only a beginning,
An eternal cycle, where no one's ever winning

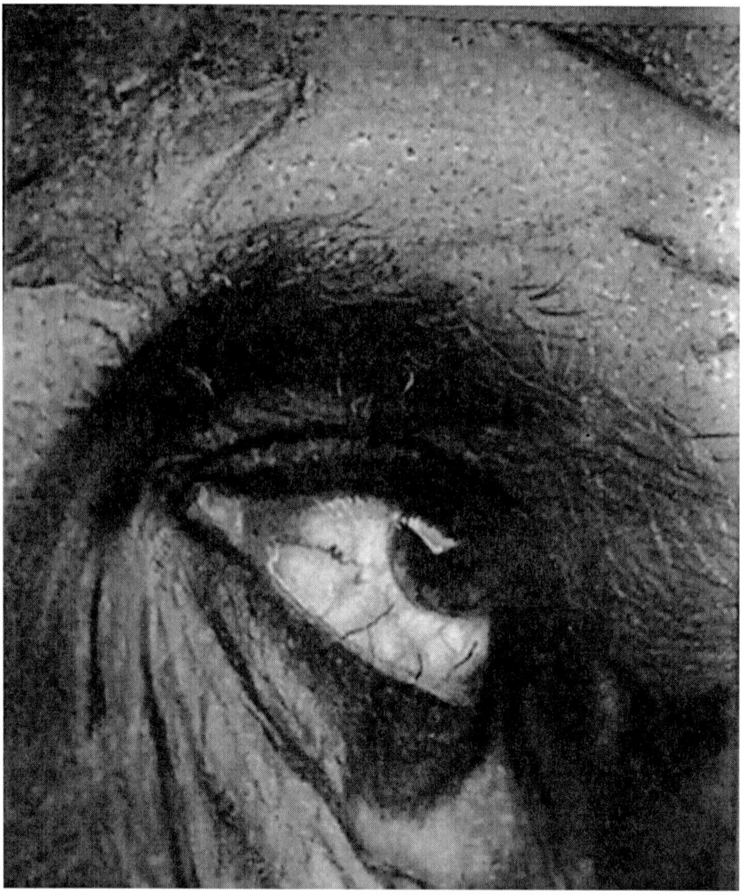

Regularity

The ghouls of regularity,

Dictate every step, referring to a prewritten invisible manual.

Immersed in polluted air,

Fogged up glasses, with no perception.

Bearing the haunted memory

Of cracking open the free will,

Only to discover nothingness.

Keep breathing the existential void,

And surrender,

For, at least, we have each other.

Lover

Love wasted, but I don't mind

Another heart break, another noise

You start where I stop

What a pity; your insomniac heart

Eager to bond;

Without risking it all,

You seek warmth when it's cold,

Your feelings are covered in snow,

I hear your music without a sound,

Your soul concealing its blue,

an illusion, just a pretence to be the

You dictated by all

Perhaps this one time, maybe, just take the fall

I'll be waiting, hit the bottom

And allow the falsehood to be forgotten

Lover 2

Your habitual outbursts

stimulate my imaginary love;

Your secret thoughts

magnify my underlying depression,

my attention structures a form out of your fantasies,

Consumed by its unknown familiarity

Is this what I've always been?

A raw naked piece of flesh,

that your mind guards to eventually feed itself?

The nude photographs that I send

in an attempt to reveal the real me

that no longer exists,

oblivious yet submissive to your misconducted symphony,

Because my love, you are my favorite tragedy

Confirmation Bias

When you try to see and look,

Justifying the truth you took.

Reality, as your mind has portrayed,

Rejecting all that might evade.

Projection, not open to a chance,

You might be wrong, give it a glance.

With no thoughts to disrupt or corrupt,

Endure the pain and the sudden abrupt.

Your eyes, like a cinematic reel,

Display your imagined drama's feel.

Slay your fears to seek reality,

Revealing clarity in its profanity

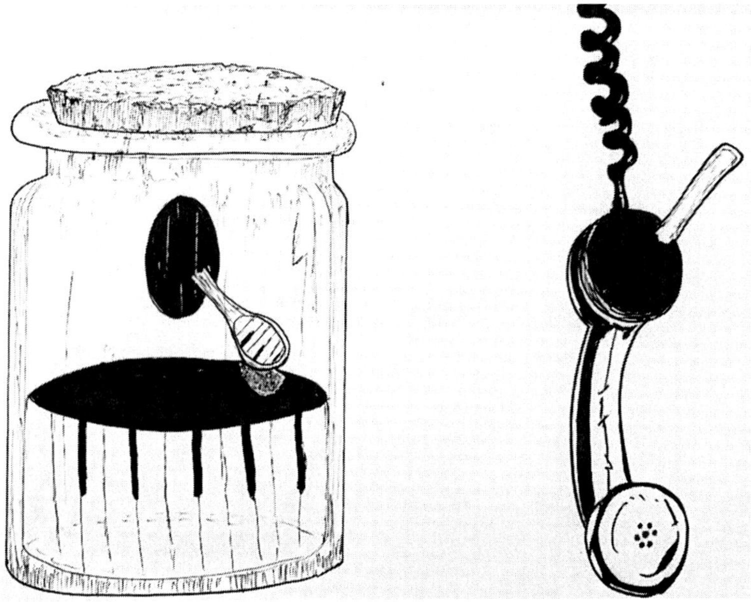

I'm all ears

I shift my focus on each pause,
as the words pour out of your mouth,
The frequency of the sound waves you make,
are no longer received by my thought

Your attempt to snatch my awareness,
To force a revolve around you like the planets;
my mind and belief now form an eclipse,
blocking your narcissistic displease

While I watch the movements your mouth makes,
cancelling out my every attempt to invade;
Can't help but wonder the need you possess,
to conceal yet establish your dominance

The vocal cord at this instance,
forgets it has a purpose to eject,
as every voice that comes out of me,
is superimposed with your synchronized tragedy

"you know what I mean?", you nudge me,

"hope you heard what I said"

"yes", I respond, while I notice your inviable mind clear,

"Like always, I'm all ears!"

Villain

Blending your emotions through a cigar,

As your blood-shot eyes were gazing into mine

I discover the monster that you truly are

Dancing on the border of your deception,

I trip, but sustain the fall;

But the faint memory of your bloody hands

succumbs me into an endless trance;

I am not a villain or a victim.

I'm the hero that defeated those hounds

You're the criminal that fled from the truth,

Disguising deceit with your wicked charm

Bully

Your mockery to conceal

insecurities that you accidentally reveal,

magnifying my flaws yet multiplying yours

Actions devoid of charm

you play your part and humiliate

I pity, deprived of hate

You win the battle of contempt

Dignity might not be a sword

but will pillow the fall,

Defeated, yet undone

Because you will always be the damaged one

Shakespeare

The crowd awaits your presence,

Eager to point out your flaws.

Stub out your cigarette in the ashtray,

Adjust your display.

Breathe in your nervousness,

Shift your focus from tragic fate, Down your last drink.

Time passes slowly if you're watching,

No saving hand to pull you through.

Everyone's pretending,

Playing hero or a victim.

It's okay to break the character's strategy,

Design your own set.

If you must be an actor,

Play the role for an audience.

Be a slow-crawling spectator,

Navigating it all.

And they can't track you down

Sober

The red lights refuse to get any dimmer,
The repetitive clinking of glasses I hear,
A warm discomfort hugs my mind's doubt,
I curse my soberness among the liquored crowd.

The bass reverberates through my body,
The dance floor seized by the dis-embodied,
A human on booze startles the sober;
I chug another drink to join the stoners.

Yet another glass fails to engulf my consciousness,
Sigh; unable to modernise my pretentiousness;
The loud music synchronises with my heartbeat,
Pledging to never present myself at these parties.

As I stood up for an out-of-body experience,
I drop on the floor and collide with the darkness.

Infinity

Have you ever found your mind wandering the infinite corridors of contemplation, exploring questions that transcend the boundaries of time and space? Amidst the digital landscape that encourages us to dissect the universe's mysteries and conspiracies, these poems become humble attempts into the abyss of inquiry.

Join me in navigating the territories of "Infinity," where verses are not just poetic expressions but humble attempts to decipher the enigmatic threads of existence. Each poem, a lantern in the cosmic darkness, seeks to illuminate the cosmic questions that stir the soul and spark the imagination.

Identity

The silenced voice,

a vision not perceived,

The potential figure of my body

or unsurfaced subconscious thought?

the truth I force to hide?

or falsity I attempt to deny?

Happiness I sabotage?

or the decisions that I do not?

Do we choose the road?

or spin the threads to be Clotho?

Are we the result of everything present?

Or of an unrecognised absence?

Music

I view your soul draw the patterns,

words that imitate your hideous senses,

I recognize this trail,

have been here for a while,

Maybe we're not alone after all;

like a river that's bound to fall,

creating a visual pleasure

veiling the echo of the pain,

you and I design a view from our ache;

you with your melody, and I as your spectator

Let's start this act again!

Melody

Your voice interrupting my thought as

I hear it mildly crack,

overtaken by music,

the vibration dominating the rest of the piece,

replicating pleasure,

with sound and some color,

product of the unknown;

the song, a mystery,

stripping down my fraudulent till core,

exhibiting our most vulnerable,

creating an army of the regulars

Imprinted

A journey into the abyss

that I volunteered to trip.

Numb throughout the fall,

with no end and a distant start.

Anticipating a change of view,

or a disconnect from the present,

generating nihilistic thoughts,

and imaginary demons for the thrill of it all.

The end seems too far,

perhaps, there is none.

All alone in the nothingness,

a move that can't be undone.

Why?

Duality of all,

comprising of rise and fall,

It's sad and happy

Life's a miracle and ordinary

It's sexual and impotent

boredom and enchantment

You're unique, also common

You're dumb and intelligent

you're beautiful and ugly

You're deprived and provided

You love, you hate

You lose, you play

Observe the entirety

you're everything you see

experience the land and flight,

Just don't ask why

Discovery

The unfamiliar, why are you out of my sight?

My dear Unknown, let's reunite,

Become my consensual expression

Share my light, and I, your darkness,

The exposed form that I previously witnessed,

How did you become my predictability?

Assemble me in a line,

to an animated land,

where the Houses have broken mirrors,

The sky reflects gray with hints of blue

Take me to an unknown land,

A place where the fish fly high

The wolves howl during the day

The cars swim in the ice

Paradise unique to its kind